Belle & Boo
and the
Birthday Surprise

Mandy Sutcliffe

ORCHARD

This is **Belle**, and this is **Boo**.

They are always together –
on sunny days,
rainy days,
and dreamy let's-be-lazy days.

One day, Belle said,

"Today is special, Boo."

"Special?" said Boo, twitching his ears. "Why?"

"It's someone's birthday. But it's a surprise whose birthday it is."

"Oh, I love surprises!" said Boo. "But what are birthdays?
  Are they nice?"

"They're very extra nice," smiled Belle. "You'll see."

She looked in her treasure box.

It was the best kind,
full of sparkly ribbons
and funny hats
and all kinds of
wonderful things.

"Are we dressing up?" Boo asked.

"Not today," said Belle. "Today, I have to make a birthday card."

Belle began to draw.

"What are you drawing?" asked Boo.

"A hug," said Belle.

"I can see it!" Boo squeaked.

"I can see the hug!"

"You can help to stick on the sparkles, Boo. Hugs need sparkles."

Boo liked sticking things.

He liked it so much
that he got stuck.

"Oh, Boo.
You'll have to wash your paws now."

Belle sang a soapy kind of song as she helped Boo to get unstuck.

"Soap and bubbles
And splish and splosh!
Boo the rabbit
Is having a wash..."

The card looked splendid.

Grrr . . . rumble

"I've got a hungry feeling inside now," sighed Boo.

"Are you very hungry, Boo?"

"Not pie and potatoes hungry," said Boo, quickly.

"Just cake and cookies hungry."

"That's good. Cake and birthdays go together."

"I like birthdays!" said Boo.

"They smell of
chocolate."

"And flowers!" said Belle.

Belle and Boo went into the garden.
Belle spread out the picnic rug
and put the plate of fairy cakes on it.

She put some daisies in an egg cup
with her card next to them.

Everything was beginning to look like
the very best kind of birthday.

There was only one thing missing . . .

"Boo?" she called.

"Boo? Where are you?"

Boo was looking in his
secret treasure place
under the oak tree.

"Here," he said, excitedly.
"Do balloons and birthdays go together?"

Boo handed Belle a bright red
balloon, all new and slippery.

"It's perfect," said Belle.

She blew

and blew

and blew

until her cheeks were red, too.

"Oh," said Boo.

"Oh, oh!"

Boo and the balloon began to float away
on a sudden puff of wind.

"Come back, Boo!"

Belle called.

"You'll miss your birthday!"

"Is it *my* birthday today?" asked Boo.

"Yes, that's the surprise! Come back for your birthday hug!"

But Boo was floating higher . . .

. . . and **higher** . . .

. . . as **high** as the oak tree.

"Help!" he called.

"Help!"

Belle climbed the ladder to the
very top of the tree house,
up and up until she
was almost dizzy.

But Belle was brave.

"Wait for me, Boo!" she called.

"Here I am!"

And she held out a long stick to Boo.

"Catch the end!" she said.

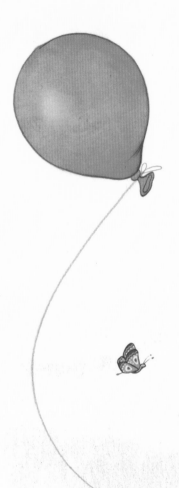

Boo reached out . . .

. . . and huffled and puffled . . .

and twizzled and whizzled . . .

until, finally, he caught hold of the stick.

Belle pulled him safely into the tree house.

"That was a surprise!" he gasped.

"I didn't know birthdays were so exciting."

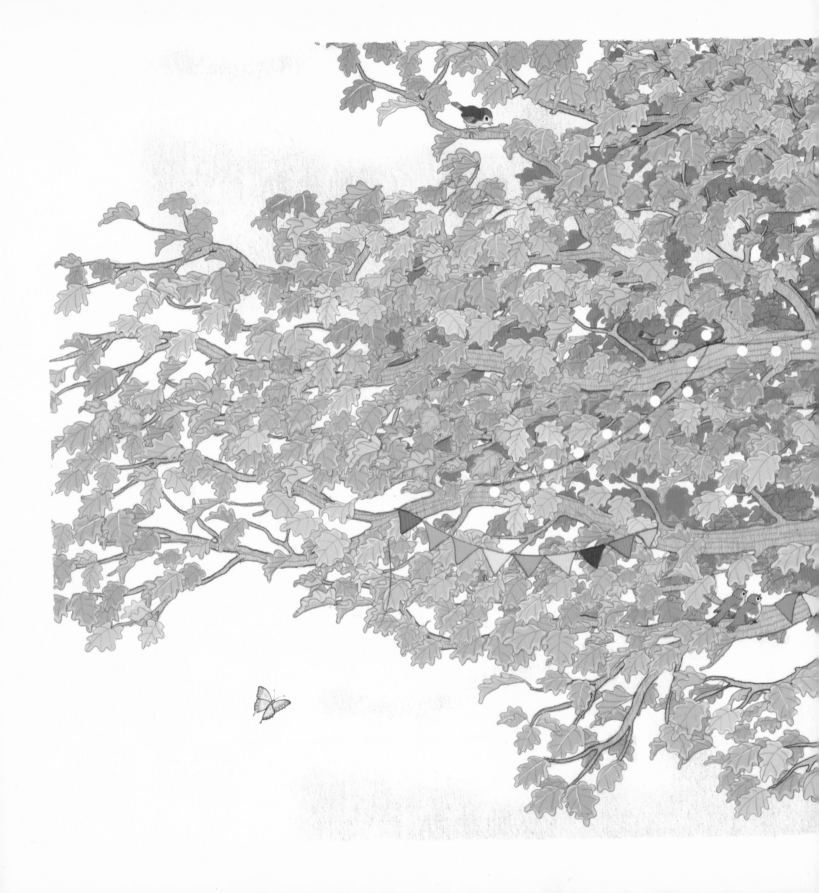

"Oh, Boo!" laughed Belle.

"Birthdays are fun!"

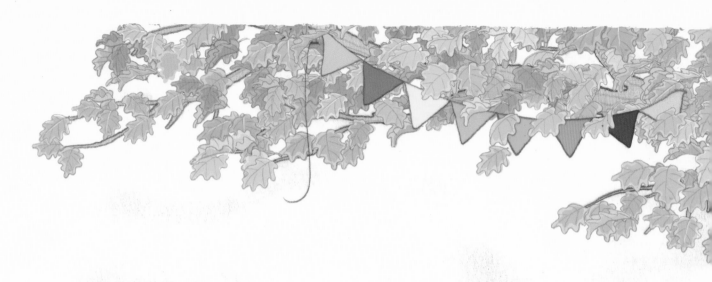

It was time for Boo's birthday picnic. Yellow Duck
and Raggedy Doll and Snuffly Elephant were there,
and everyone had fun and ate lots of cakes.
Then Belle sang a birthday kind of song for Boo.

"Happy Birthday to Boo,
The rabbit who flew,
Happy Birthday, Happy Birthday!
And Boo, I love you."

"Birthdays are the best," said Boo.
"And I think you're even better than birthdays,"
said Belle, giving Boo a very special birthday hug.

This Book Belongs To

. . . .

To all our Belle and Boo friends who have supported us from the very beginning thank you

ORCHARD BOOKS
338 Euston Road, London NW1 3BH
Orchard Books Australia
Level 17/207 Kent Street, Sydney, NSW 2000

First published in 2012 by Orchard Books
First published in paperback in 2012

ISBN 978 1 40831 609 2

Text by Gillian Shields
Text © Orchard Books 2012
Illustrations © Mandy Sutcliffe 2012

The right of Mandy Sutcliffe to be identified as the illustrator of this work
has been asserted by her in accordance with the Copyright, Designs and Patents Act, 1988.

A CIP catalogue record for this book is available from the British Library.

1 3 5 7 9 10 8 6 4 2

Printed in China

Orchard Books is a division of Hachette Children's Books,
an Hachette UK company.
www.hachette.co.uk